THE VEGETABLES GO TO BED

BY Christopher King

ILLUSTRATED BY Mary GrandPré

CROWN PUBLISHERS, INC. ◆ New York

Published by Crown Publishers, Inc.,
a Random House company, 201 East 50th Street,
New York, New York 10022

CROWN is a trademark of Crown Publishers, Inc.

Manufactured in Singapore

Library of Congress Cataloging-in-Publication Data
King, Christopher, 1945–
The vegetables go to bed / by Christopher L. King ;
illustrated by Mary GrandPré.
Summary: The tomatoes, carrots, spinach plants,
and other vegetables in the garden prepare to go
to bed, each in its own fashion.
1. Bedtime–Fiction. 2. Vegetables–Fiction. 3.
Stories in rhyme.] I. Grandpre, Mary, ill. II. Title.
PZ8.3K568Ve 1994
[E]–dc20   92-27650

ISBN 0-517-59125-1 (trade)
0-517-59126-X (lib. bdg.)

10 9 8 7 6 5 4 3 2 1   First Edition

For Chitra,
my favorite gardening partner.

C. K.

To Mom and Dad
and the Hawka-bird and
Chincha-bug.

M. G.

Shhh! The vegetables are going to bed.

Every pea and carrot,

Cabbage, bean, and brussels sprout

Will be tucked in

Before the stars come out.

Plump tomatoes wash their ruddy cheeks with dew,

And so should you.

Cornstalks in the evening rain have bathed their tender ears.

Corncobs snuggle up in corn silk

Till the sun appears.

But lettuces are restless and won't say the day is done,

Until the summer wind has come

And gently kissed each one.

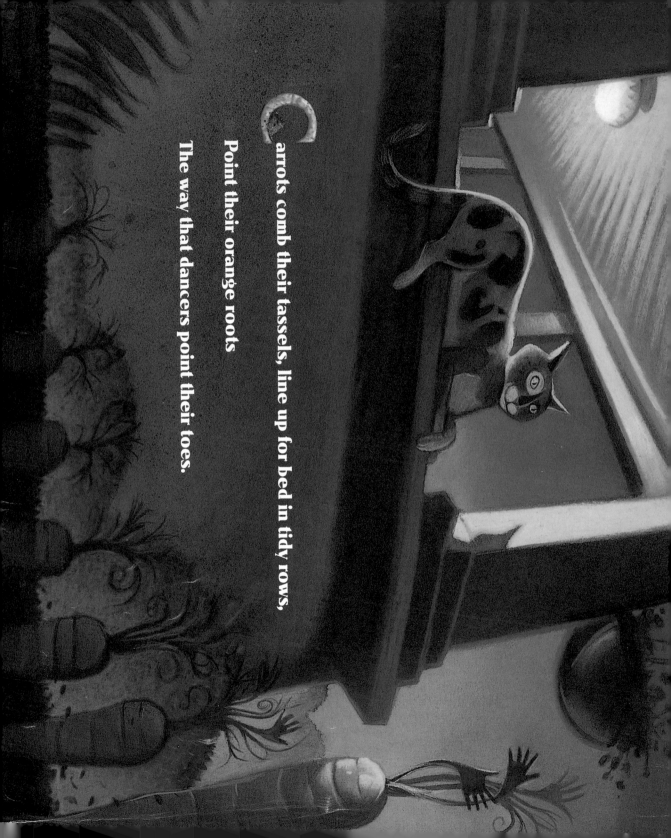

Carrots comb their tassels, line up for bed in tidy rows,
Point their orange roots
The way that dancers point their toes.

The onions have been crying:

"We don't want to go to sleep."

But they're nice and cozy now

And much too tired to weep.

ne by one, potatoes close their eyes,

Listening to the sound of bells,

The peppers' lullabies.

Sleepy spinach plants give one last wave with leafy hands,

Before they drift away

To dreams of wild green wonderlands.

All around the garden, the marigolds stand guard.

No hungry bug or beetle

Dares steal into their yard.

Outside your window,

The sun turns off the light.

Good night, you vegetables.

Good night! Good night!